Nights in the
Iron Hotel

MICHAEL HOFMANN

Nights in the
Iron Hotel

faber and faber

LONDON · BOSTON

First published in 1983
by Faber and Faber Limited
3 Queen Square London WC1N 3AU
Filmset by Wilmaset, Birkenhead, Merseyside
Printed in Great Britain by
Whitstable Litho Limited, Whitstable, Kent
All rights reserved

British Library Cataloguing in Publication Data

Hofmann, Michael
  Nights in the Iron Hotel.
  I. Title
  821'.914   PR6058.0/

  ISBN 0-571-13116-6

Library of Congress Cataloging in Publication Data

Hofmann, Michael, 1957–
  Nights in the iron hotel.

  I. Title.
PR6058.0345N5   1984   821'.914   83-11675
ISBN 0-571-13116-6 (pbk.)

Contents

Acknowledgements

Grateful acknowledgement is made to the *Agni Review*, BBC Radio 3, *Encounter*, Hutchinson Books Ltd/Arts Council, *Listener, London Magazine, London Review of Books, New Statesman, PN Review, Poetry Review, Quarto, Straight Lines, The Times Literary Supplement, Twofold*.

'*Hausfrauenchor*' was a runner-up in the 1980 Arvon Competition. 'White Noise' first appeared in *Poetry*, 'Fates of the Expressionists' in *American Scholar*.

Looking at You   (Caroline)

Having your photograph on my bedside table
is like having a propeller there . . . My friend
did his project on the Gallipoli Offensive—
with a proud Appendix of family heirlooms:
irrelevant fragments of German aircraft.
I covered the Russian Revolution (the only
lasting consequence of the Great War,
I argued) but with nothing more tactile
than a picture section—central feeding
in tsarist times: cabbage soup and black bread,
the Eisenstein-faced peasants with red pupils . . .
I take your unnaturally serious expression
and coax it into a smile or a glum look—
dotted lines pencilled in for velocity—but
you still won't budge. Then I imagine your
stasis as whir, movement in perfect phase,
just before it starts walking backwards . . .
All the walks here lead into the autobahn:
they are dual carriageways for pedestrians,
with wire bridges over traffic unusually
quiet in the snow. A blue signpost marks
the distances: Nürnberg 100; Würzburg
(home of the Volkswagen) 200; Berlin 500 . . .

The pioneers of aviation were never alone—
they named their machines after their loved ones.

Dependants

These specks of metal on my hands: gold dust,
or the lead we accumulate that kills us?
I have put off your visit this week, and watch
the late movie on TV, alone with my regrets . . .

The searchlight is a romantic theatre moon.
It makes the rounds of the prison, bathes it
in a blue glow, then swivels off across the bay . . .
The inmates wear denim and sleep six to a room.

They share a girl on a calendar, her pout
a vague ecstasy that recalls a wife or girlfriend
to each of them. In their interminable nights,
they climb the moonbeams and cross to the mainland

of their memories, the love that led them astray
with its dreams of mediocrity and comfort.
Her upturned face, framed by expensive furs . . .
Now they meet once a month, through a grille.

The initiative is with those on the outside:
a wife's assurances; a lawyer come to say
that divorce proceedings are being instituted;
the file slipped into a home-made birthday cake.

Diablerie

Your ringed hands clutch your elbows. In your arms
is someone else's child, a black-eyed baby girl
dressed like His Satanic Majesty in a red romper suit:
a gleeful crustacean, executing pincer movements.

Day in the Netherlands

Commuting tourists, we retire
from the city in the evening
to a house in the floral suburbs,
Linnaeuslaan, the street sign giving
the dates of the great botanist . . .

From the fibreglass perfection
of a fly-boat, we saw Amsterdam's
thinnest house; prison-cells built into
the supports of a bridge, their
window-bars called Swedish curtains

on the German commentary tape;
the station constructed on thousands
of wooden piles. The Shell building—
that funny look in its windows
comes from the gold dust in them . . .

We are so overfed that if we
had supper as well, we could
only quarrel afterwards. So we
skip it and sit by the canal
in the last warmth of the year.

For the first time, we dare to talk
about our past, contiguity that
preceded love, and kept it
at bay . . . My room opened off yours,
it could have been a cupboard.

Touring Company

In your cavalier fashion, you leave your
small change on my floor. You keep pots of it
at home.—It feels sick to be alone again.
Like a charlady I shake my head at the dust,
and scrape it into pieces of knitting
with my fingers.—On the *Nautilus* there was
apparently never any dust, as all their air
came out of cylinders. But then Strindberg
or Hamsun, or another of those northern mis-
anthropes, writes that dust consists almost
entirely of dead human skin . . . Captain
Nemo's men can't have decomposed as we do.

Yesterday, you played five small male parts
in *Macbeth*: four cowards and a murdered child—
a friend drew a red line across your throat
with his dagger. I sat in the front row,
worrying about the psychological consequences
of being murdered every night for a month . . .
And the blood seeped into our private life;
that of the stars was washable, but yours was
permanent for economy. It pales on my sheets,
souvenir of your lovely blush . . . When you left,
you forgot your vanishing-cream—my biker,
spark-plugs mixing with tampons in your handbag!

First Night

Electrodes attached to a flautist's cheeks:
a measure of nerves, his fear of the performance.

You move the fifty-seven muscles it takes to smile.
It's strange to see you again. A faint tan

is like dust on your memory, a shade or two,
numbers along the spectrum of available paints . . .

A freshness about your eyes suggests you are
newly hatched, like Eve, in an unfamiliar world.

I cross my legs, and watch the twitch of reflex—
Plato's great longing, my foot helplessly kicking space

Miracles of Science

"I had made a religion of his will,
the Papal Bull of his Infallibility . . .
He chose for both of us, and I was happy.

Three bags full. He had an affair
and told me. That he was impelled to it
by loneliness and a long curiosity.

How can I forget it? They got drunk,
had sex, and lay in bed watching TV.
It's as obvious as though I'd done it myself.

An alien nerve attached to the body
of our experience. He planted it, that part
I keep rejecting. His pleasure hurts me.

In seven years, after the cellular renewal
of my body,
                    I will be a different person."

A Feminist Ballet

The colour in life is supplied by women . . .
She bought a pair of baggy workman's overalls,
cut them up, & dyed the pieces separately
in all the colours of the rainbow: Roy G. Biv.

Thomas Mann's Aschenbach, a stream of ashes,
longed for the arrival of his dinner-suit,
a uniform of moral & cultural stability,
the belief in an unimpeachable Absolute.

(When he started wearing younger clothes,
rouged his cheeks, & painted his lips like
sickly twin cherries, he was only making
things easier for the mortuary beautician.)

So it is with the captains of German industry;
an aerial photograph shows them in small groups,
one hand nursing a drink, the other in a roomy
trouser-pocket. Over their hearts, they wear

handkerchiefs impeccable as their credentials.
Like anarchists, they see things in black & red.
—A society closed to women, they stand on
the solid ground of a brightly submissive carpet.

Museum Piece

The room smells of semen. The leather curtain
that hangs in the doorway to keep the men
from the boys is now flapping like a ventilator . . .
People crowd in to see the erotic drawings.
Yonis in close-up like a row of fingerprints.
—Hokusai's hairfine precipice technique
applied to pubic hair. Fingers do the walking,
tiny feet wave in mid-air. His white ladies
groan under the weight of swollen members.
. . . The four estates of Japanese society—
fishermen, actors, courtesans and samurai—
mixing it. Following no useful calling,
anonymous in their nakedness, lovers clutch
each other. We might be watching ourselves,
dizzy men and women without designations . . .
We jostle in the dark for a better view.

Mannequin

Somewhere between a health-food store
and a DIY Centre—the sex shop.
Six inches of plastic are on display
in the window, a bust of the Venus de Milo.

(An emblem of passive non-resistance,
like Gandhi's Indians lying down
under railway trains: slippery Houdinis
in the great cliff-hanger of the dusty plains.)

A foolproof bondage for the connoisseur.

Entropy   (The Late Show)

A split screen, the dream of the early cineastes,
who rounded on their audiences and assaulted them
with pandemonium in a dip- or triptych, shooting
that all-time favourite, the end of the world.
Screaming crowds ensured a box-office success.
People paid to watch themselves and their own
futuristic hysteria in the huge convex mirrors
held up to them in the cinemas of the avant-garde.
They are the antecedents of today's disaster movie
(especially blooming in Japan), and also of this:

. game of darts. On the right half of the screen,
completely expressionless, the pot-bellied players.
Standing like storks on one leg, they lean forward
behind their heavy throwing-arm. Some of them use
a little finger as a telescopic sight. They practise
six or seven hours a day . . . On the left, in close-up,
their target, treble twenty. With the best of them,
the margin of error is an eighth of an inch, a letter
in type.
        Hating numbers, they rattle down to zero.

In Connemara

This country has shaken off its
inhabitants and filled their fields
with water and stones. Between
outraged wavings of the grass,
sullen pools like thick dark eyes
ignore us. The ground breathes
proudly through its clotted pelts.
A granular light hurls brittle stars
against our faces. We stand at last
on the panting hills, where the wind
tightens its cries and blows them away.

Extinction

So now, after twenty-six years, he hangs up
and walks out on you. The line goes dead
as you tell me. Electricity cheeps and thrills—
a malfunction at some international exchange.

There wasn't time to offer sympathy or advice,
not that I knew what to say, in any case . . .
Your life has been one attrition, and when you try
clumsily to defend your interests, he snaps back:

"Forward my mail, I'm not coming home again."
For him, as for the Old Man of the Sea,
there's always someone else, another willing back
to climb. But when you're a woman, past fifty,

with a family and no career, what then . . . ?
Flat earth, the narrative curve of dusk.
A string of lights indicates the road that
brings people to this place. The rip of canvas

as pigeons scatter in terror from their branches.
A faraway siren sounds like faint breathing.
From the middle of a field, the plaintive
squeak of some low and resilient life-form . . .

Myopia in Rupert Brooke Country

Birds, feathers, a few leaves, flakes of soot—
things start to fall. The stubble has been burned,
and the fields are striped in black and gold.
Elsewhere, the hay is still drying on long racks:
bulky men prancing about on slender hooves,
unconvincing as pantomime cattle . . . A hedgehog
lies rolled over on its side like a broken castor.
Abandoned in one corner is a caravan that has
not been on holiday all year. Forever England . . .
A hot-air balloon sinks towards the horizon—
the amateur spirit or an advertising gimmick?
Quickly flames light it up, the primitive roar
of a kitchen geyser, and its calcified heart
gives a little skip, then slides down like tears.

White Noise

It blows your mind,

the radio, or whatever piece of sonic equipment
you keep along with the single white rose
and the spiked mirror in your monochrome room . . .
I've seen it through the open door sometimes.

You hoover twice a week, and in my eyes
that amounts to a passion for cleanliness.
The vacuum, its pre-war drone in the corridor.
Thin and snub-nosed, a gas-mask on a stick.

Your reveille is at six: you go downstairs
for a glass of water with your vitamin pills.
Then back to your room, and your light stays on
till late.—What do you do to kill the time?

. . . Trailing cigarette smoke and suspicion,
you prowl through the house, accident-prone
and painfully thin in your sepulchral clothes.
Reality filters through your tinted spectacles.

And in the afternoon, your looped-tape excesses:
a couple of pop standards in your repertoire,
the demonstration piece for synthesizer,
and that thrilling concerto for nose-flute . . .

Two floors away, I can still hear the storm.
The jungle and the platitudes of sentiment
battle it out with technology, sweep you
into a corner of your room, delirious, trembling,

a pile of leaves.

Hausfrauenchor

"She's younger than I am, almost certainly
blonde, and he sleeps with her once a year . . .
The occasion is the office-party—alcohol,
music, and their formal routine collaboration
suddenly becomes something else.—All over
the country, wives write to the agony columns
for advice. One letter covers thousands
of cases. Of course, you want to allow him
his bit of fun; after working all year for
Germany's *Wirtschaftswunder* and your own.
And it's probably more than you can provide
with your cooking, your meat-and-two-veg sex,
the occasional *Sauerbraten* . . . He deserves it.
The rest of the time, he's faithful to you.
But when he comes home at some godforsaken hour,
lipstuck and dishevelled, drunk as a god, his
dried sperm crackling and flaking in his pants,
then you feel differently about it. You wish
you'd gone to the party and kept an eye on him.
—But then the newspapers don't recommend that:
husbands resent it—what's your business
in an office where you never set foot otherwise?
They tell you the only course is to declare
a general amnesty for this particular offence.
A mass-exemption, like the students of '68,
who no longer have a 'past', and instead hold
positions in the Civil Service: vetting radicals;
checking over photographs of demonstrations,
signatories on petitions; looking for traces
of the ineradicable red paint that is sprayed
over crowds of Communists to identify them . . .

So the best way is to kill them with kindness.
—And it isn't any easier for the secretary:
because she doesn't want to be a cock-teaser,
she gets into trouble with her boyfriend . . .
A week or two later, she gives my husband a tie
for Christmas. The whole family (himself
included) make fun of it, a silly pattern,
awful colours, what a useless garment anyway . . .
But then he wears it all the following year."

In the Amazon

after Mario Vargas Llosa

Sad, these weddings. The love between man and woman
is water under the bridge, water under the motorboat . . .
A track through the jungle, carved by a machete knife,
will last only a few hours. Rivers are the only roads,
and they change course so quickly, maps are obsolete.

. . . The Amazon was named after its warm-blooded fishes
with breasts like mermaids, hung up to die. The Spaniards
thought they were women, and justified their own cruelty.
The river is the River of Life. Nothing keeps on its banks.
Plants, insects and disease—the great chain of being.

The nuns prepare a snack: papaya juice and *petits fours*.
—Why get married anyway, when she isn't even pregnant?
And yet they are stern, and deal out admonitions . . .
Within a few years, injustice has caught up with him,
while she is having the children of some relation of his.

—What is love? Men are like flies. She has to eat.

Pavement Artistes

after E. L. Kirchner

His women are birds of paradise, cocottes:
stiletto-heeled, smoking, dressed to kill.
They wear veils to cage the savagery

of their features. Like the motherly pelican,
they are plucked bare—except their hats,
which are feathered and tipped like arrows.

They live together on a green traffic island.
Berlin Zoologischer Garten—*tristes tropiques*!
The station clock measures their allurements.

Their control of outlying stairways and arches
is ensured by their human architecture.
The gothic swoop of shoulder, waist and hip.

For men, they are something of a touchstone,
distinguishing them into the two categories
of policeman and clown . . . You can see both types

strolling down the boulevard, bowler-hatted
and terrified of shadows—sometimes testing
the street's temperature with a long foot.

Gruppenbild ohne Dame

1923, gathering Depression. In this interior
in Cologne, it's Laocöon all over again.
This time, Fate has left him his two boys
and taken his wife.—Though it is difficult
to see how a woman could have fitted in, here:
a road winding in an empty landscape on the wall,
the threadbare carpet, and one hard Sunday chair.
. . . A male Trinity, the Father and his two Sons.
The maculate conceptions of his bald head.
Baby watchchains like Papa's, and knickerbockers
aspiring to the condition of his three-piece suit.
Their knotty skulls show a family likeness,
heads shaved for lice and summer—skinny boys
with their mother's big eyes and hurt mouth.

Family Holidays

The car got a sun-tan while my father worked
in its compound . . . Mixed with the cicadas,
you could hear the fecundity of his typing
under the green corrugated plastic roof.

My mother staggered about like a nude
in her sun-hat, high heels and bathing-costume.
She was Quartermaster and Communications.

My doughy sisters baked on the stony beach,
swelling out of their bikinis, turning over
every half-hour. Still, they were never done.

The little one fraternized with foreign children.

. . . Every day I swam further out of my depth,
but always, miserably, crawled back to safety.

The Magic of Mantovani

for Simon Korner

The invited audience applauds on cue—
steady couples in their late twenties,
well-dressed and supplied with contraceptives.

A giant in the world of light music, they say;
so much happiness in those globe-trotting tunes . . .
The surf of percussion. Swaying in treetops,

violins hold the high notes. Careful brass
for the darker moments—the blood of Spain.
The accordion is a European capital . . .

A sentimental music, porous with associations,
it played in the dimness before the ads,
when I went to the cinema with my father.

He disappeared into his own thoughts, abstracted,
rubbing his fingers together under his nose . . .
Scattered in the red plush of the cinema,

a handful of people were waiting for the feature.
Regular constellations of stars twinkled
on the ceiling while daylight wasted outside.

Ice-cream was no longer on sale in the foyer—
the end of kindness . . . I thought about mortality,
and cried for my father's inevitable death.

Boys' Own

A parting slightly off-centre, like Oscar Wilde's,
his fat mouth, and the same bulky appearance.
Your hair was pomaded, an immaculate wet-look,
sculpted and old-fashioned in these blow-dry times.
The dull grain of wood on polished furniture.
—Everyone has an inspiring English teacher
somewhere behind them, and you were ours. We argued
about you: that your smell was not sweet after-shave,
but the presbyterian rigours of cold water—

on your porous face and soft, womanish hands . . . ?
The public-school teacher has to be versatile—
if not the genuine Renaissance article, then at least
a modern pentathlete—and so you appeared to us
in as many guises as an Action Man: for lessons,
with a gown over one of your heavy three-piece suits;
wearing khaki for Corps on Wednesday afternoons;
as a soccer referee in a diabolical black tracksuit;
in baggy but respectable corduroys on holidays . . .

Morning coffee was followed by pre-prandial sherry
after only the shortest of intervals. The empties,
screw-tops, stood in boxes outside your door.
You drank early, copiously, and every day—
though it hardly crossed our minds. Given the chance,
we would have done too . . . It was "civilized",
and that was what you were about. Sweet and sour sherry,
lager on warm afternoons, the pathos of sparkling wine
for occasions. "It's actually quite like champagne . . ."

Just as an extension-lead went from your gramophone
to its little brother, a "stereophonic" loudspeaker—
Ferguson Major and Minor . . . With one hand in your
                                                    pocket,
leaning back in your swivelling chair, you conducted
your own records, legs double-crossed like Joyce's.
—Among all those other self-perpetuating oddball
bachelors, how could we fail to understand you?
Your military discipline and vintage appearance,
the sublimation of your Anglicanism, your drinking . . .

We only waited for that moment at the end of a class,
when, exhausted by intellectual inquiry, you took off
your glasses and rubbed away your tiny blue eyes . . .
All of love and death can be found in books;
you would have agreed. At one of your gatherings,
someone found a pubic hair in your sheepskin rug . . .
Years later, there was a scandal, an ultimatum,
and you threw yourself under the wheels of a train—
the severe way Tolstoy chose for Anna Karenina.

Universal Uncles

The two men—forties, balding, brothers—
live together in a couple of rooms downstairs.
With them are two children, under-tens:
a girl, and a boy who isn't quite right . . .
They are either half-siblings or Benjamins,
late additions to the family of the men's parents.
They are a cosy group, the children have
a pretty good time. The men take trouble
over them, they have an affectionate nature . . .
They took my little sister to the playground.
It had been raining, and they played a game,
jumping her over puddles, and after each one
giving her a kiss. Some time, the puddles stop
but not the kissing . . . On warm Saturdays,
they wash their battered, field-grey Mercedes,
and take their charges for a drive in the country.
—Next to the two round stereo loudspeakers
in the back window are their twin straw hats,
the type that donkeys wear on the beach.

Young Werther

The petrol-pump attendants in Yugoslavia
still wear your livery—yellow T-shirt
and blue dungarees. But they leave it at that,
avoiding the further symptoms of your decline:
the habit of pouring your life into a diary;
your inordinate self-pity; a proneness to
seasonal ailments, which, taken in conjunction
with your pantheism, was to prove fatal . . .
What really killed you was autumn. The leaves.
Likewise your foolish generation of virgins,
who followed you, then Napoleon, in everything.
Liebestod all over Europe, a messy business.
Did Art ever again affect Life to that degree?
The unacknowledged legislator of ducks' tails,
Beatle-mania, mini-skirts, glue-sniffing,
snuff movies . . .

                        And over there,
shinning back up the cliff, visibly ageing,
Goethe on his way to conversations with Eckermann;
dandling little Bettina—at sixteen no longer
a child—on his knee; mutual appreciation with
Lord Byron; a future as an abominable father.

Migrations of an Older Romantic

Whenever he felt sad, he headed for the Rhine
and made a conquest of one of the maidens.
It was his heartland: he loved the vineyards
on the slopes, the endless railway tunnels,
the coal barges going to Switzerland and back.

—His women were scarcely into their teens;
they were "von" this or "von" that, but they had
Enlightenment Christian names like Esther or Clara.
They remembered him for the rest of their lives.
These hectic love-affairs broke up his loneliness

and briefly injected him with the enthusiasm
he found so hard to come by any more. The opiate
of underage Muses. Recidivism for the sake of
inspiration. Though the songs that came out of it
were, in his late manner, drab and pietistic.

Rather absurdly, he would dedicate them to those
water-nymphs, his quick geographical mistresses.
And if they were lucky, he'd write them a letter
as well, informing them that they hadn't ever
really understood him; but then, nobody did . . .

Sometimes he even admitted that they had failed
to match the impression of his very first visit
to their arterial river—in their parents' time,
a generation ago. With a fellow poet and fabulist,
his bosom friend and future brother-in-law,

who had done the right thing and died young . . .

The Nomad, my Father

Fused with your car, a modern centaur,
you commute to work like the Tartar hordes
who swept across Europe, drinking their mares' milk.

Half the week in a neighbouring country,
then, laden with spoils, home to your smoky tents.
Your sulky children, long-haired and murderous,

help you unpack. Crates of soda water,
plastic sacks of meat . . . A hard currency buys
the cheap produce of the paper economies.

After your deprived childhood, the next few days
are a glut, a race against putrefaction . . .
And then it's time for you to go away again.

Once there was a bureaucratic inquiry
to determine where you should be registered.
What was the centre of your life-interests?

You said your family; your family said your work.

Love on the Rocks

The young man climbed out of the sea, dripping.
He had a beautiful body. The king's daughter
did not resist him. The love stirred inside her.
Then he returned to the sea, and she to her maidens
and the housework . . . Later she founded a city.

The song was so ancient that even the French girls
could not understand it. (But they were landlocked,
from Strasbourg.) They hummed the nasal tune,
and declared that you lost all the romanticism anyway
in translation, and kept only the pornographic aspect.

There was onion soup with bread and cheese in it,
flambée with rum. When everyone had gone, we decided
to clear up. The girl put on her dancing shoes,
rested one foot on top of the other, and started
washing the plates.—I was given a dishcloth.

Lord B. and Others

Yoghurt and garlic pills, Balkan products
that feed on the myth of immortality
in South-Eastern Europe; based on
the continuing survival of generations
of gypsy violinists and fortune-tellers
born before the birth certificate . . .
A weather-beaten old gent on a poster
in a chemist's shop; glaring; below him,
his ambiguous life-enhancing statement:
"It's not how old you are that matters,
it's how old you feel." Crossing the Alps,
the spectre of Shelley's sister-in-law
following him, pregnant with his child,
Byron stopped at an inn and surrendered
his passport; then entered name and address
on the printed form, giving his age as
"a hundred". When he died, eight years later,
still only thirty-six, his heart and brain
were accordingly found to be quite used up—
"those of an old man", a devout particular
in his French romancier's biography.

By Forced Marches

Who knows what would happen if you stopped?
The autobiography draws out, lengthens
towards the end. Life stays in one place,
often Rome; and to compensate, you cut up
your time in many pieces. Rations are halved,
then quartered. The emergency is acute.
Now it is one lump of sugar per day.

l'an trentiesme de son eage

Côte d'Azur, 1919

Ospedaletti. The little hospitals—
a makeshift sanatorium for one,
despite a wicked climate of cold and wind.
A few miles down the coast, the weather
is far milder—the French Riviera just then
coming into fashion: Monte Carlo, Nice,
Menton with its Mansfield memorial . . .
St Tropez was a fishing-port until
Brigitte Bardot put it on the map,
years later, by going around topless.
K. M. has TB. With her is "L. M.", alias
Ida Baker. K. M. criticizes her incessantly—
one disagreeable feature of her illness.
It's hardly the scandalous lesbian affair
you read about, but a sad, bitchy one . . .
Her spendthrift nature; no intellectual
or personal stimulus to be got from her;
the sheer banality of her appearance—
her tiny blind breasts, her baby mouth,
the underlip always wet and a crumb or two
or a chocolate stain at the corners . . .
God knows there are enough adversities besides.
—The gardener is a rogue: charging extra
for flowers he promised to supply free.
Like everything else, they are for Murry,
her husband. They have never really lived
together. She wants to lure him back to her,
but he is in England, advancing his career
as a man of letters . . . She wrote to him,
I love you more than ever now I am 31.

Shapes of Things

We are living in the long shadow of the Bomb—
a fat Greenpeace whale, simplified and schematic
like the sign "lavatories for the handicapped",
its whirling genitals a small outboard swastika . . .

I saw the rare Ava Gardner, the last woman alive,
modelling her check workshirts in *On the Beach*.
As the wind drove the heavy clouds of fallout
towards them, there were no ugly scenes of anarchy—

only revivalist preachers and the Salvation Army band . .
She admired the *esprit de corps* of her husband
as he went down in the last living submarine—
an obsolete nuclear cigar, doused in the bay.

Fürth i. Wald

for Jan and Anja T.

There are seagulls inland, extensive flooding
and a grey sky. A tractor stalled in midfield
between two goals. Mammoth sawmills collecting trees
and pulping them for furniture and wallpaper . . .
These strips of towns, with their troubled histories,
they are lost in the woods like Hansel and Gretel.
Counters at peace conferences, they changed hands
so often, they became indistinguishable, worthless.
Polyglot and juggled like Belgium, each of them keeps
a spare name in the other language to fall back on.
Only their wanton, spawning frontier tells them apart,
an arrogant line of wire in an electric clearing.
(A modern derivative of the civic myth of Thebes:
the oxhide cut into ribbons by cunning estate agents,
and laid end to end; so many towns called Cuernavaca . . .)
—At other frontiers, it may be a long tunnel instead,
too long for you to hold your breath. At halfway,
the texture of the concrete changes, and the lights,
but you can't say where it is brighter or safer . . .
Nations are irregular parcels, tight with fear.
But their contents have settled during transport.
Grenzflucht. Perimeters that are now deserted and
timid, the dream-wrappings clash with each other.
On one side, the lonely heartless villas of the guards.
Dustbins stored like sandbags outside barrackrooms.
The play of searchlights . . . On the other, *Der Neue
Tag* dawns only twice a week nowadays. With its
Nazi-sounding name and millenarian ideals, still
holding the fort for a dwindling readership . . .

On Fanø

Acid rain from the Ruhr strips one pine in three . . .
To supplement their living, the neutral Danes
let out their houses during the summer months—
exposure, convexity, clouds and the shadows of clouds.
Wild grass grows on the manure of their thatch.

There are concrete bunkers among the sand dunes—
bomb shelters, or part of Heligoland and the V2s . . . ?
German hippies have taken them over, painted them
with their acid peace dreams; a cave art of
giant people, jungles, a plague of dragonflies.

Fates of the Expressionists

The Kaiser was the first cousin of George V,
descended, as he was, from *German* George,
and unhappy Albert, the hard-working Saxon Elector.
—The relaxed, navy-cut beard of the one,
hysterical, bristling moustaches of the other . . .
The Expressionists were Rupert Brooke's generation.
Their hold on life was weaker than a baby's.
Their deaths, at whatever age, were infant mortality—
a bad joke in this century. Suddenly become sleepy,
they dropped like flies, whimsical, sizzling,
ecstatic, from a hot light-bulb. Even before the War,
Georg Heym and a friend died in a skating accident.
From 1914, they died in battle and of disease—
or suicide like Trakl. *Drugs Alcohol Little Sister.*
One was a student at Oxford and died, weeks later,
on the other side . . . Later, they ran from the Nazis.
Benjamin was turned back at the Spanish border—
his history of the streets of Paris unfinished—
deflected into an autistic suicide. In 1938,
Ödön von Horváth, author of naturalistic comedies,
was struck by a falling tree. In Paris.
                                        At the time
my anthology was compiled, there were still a few left:
unexplained survivors,
                        psychoanalysts in the New World.

A Western Pastoral

"There are thirty or forty other characters—
poor people mostly, and my enemies. Sometimes
I wish I had their spirit, but I'm not a man
of action. It's my money that works for me.
Ambition is its only weakness. Utopianism.
Trying to turn gritty farmers into flunkeys;
their dirt farms into an Oasis of Fun—complete
with eighteen-hole golfcourse, drive-ins,
amusement parks, motels, swimming-pools built
like busty women . . . But I came into conflict
with the sentimental forces of social thought:
conservation, minority rights, local heritage . . .
I document the loss of life force (*libido*)
in the rancher. That's how my family began—
as cattle farmers owning huge slabs of Arizona
and enough feudal gunmen to protect their skins.
. . . If my grandfather fancied anyone, he just
cut their throats and fucked them. Indio women.
No fear of litigation: they were his chattels.
A man's property he could treat as he liked.
. . . I married a woman I found in New Orleans.
She's the quiet kind, a luscious blonde—
all soft with drinking like plums in brandy.
Under the stars, after a business reversal,
she puts her head in my lap and empties me."

Nights in the Iron Hotel

Our beds are at a hospital distance.
I push them together. Straw matting
on the walls produces a Palm Beach effect:

long drinks made with rum in tropical bars.
The position of mirror and wardrobe
recalls a room I once lived in happily.

Our feelings are shorter and faster now.
You confess a new infidelity. This time,
a trombone player. His tender mercies . . .

All night, we talk about separating.
The radio wakes us with its muzak.
In a sinister way, you call it lulling.

We are fascinated by our own anaesthesia,
our inability to function. Sex is a luxury,
an export of healthy physical economies.

The TV stays switched on all the time.
Dizzying social realism for the drunks.
A gymnast swings like a hooked fish.

Prague

Tales from Chekhov

They are in a hotel in a foreign country
where the morals are different. It is their
first time away from home, and it is not
going well. He, as a leading industrialist,
has implosion on his mind: the destruction
of their vacuum by the external pressures
of this place—the laughter and fertility,
arrogant *machismo*, spicy cooking. He hopes
his British restraint will see him through . . .
But there are internal forces to contend with
as well. Their marriage has crept safely past
its "accursed seventh year"—without children.
. . . Husband and wife fall back on each other.
He obscurely feels and resents foreign blood
in her; it allows her to feel at home here,
in this ruined, pregnant city—and keeps her
from understanding him. He becomes cynical.
Other women he sees begin to look attractive . . .
but he gets nowhere. Meanwhile, she discovers
the extinct possibilities that every woman has
in her past—and mournfully explores them.

Their respective tourism exhausts them both.
He helps her downstairs with his knuckle cocked
against the small of her back like a trigger.
It is a last, sarcastic form of etiquette.
—Ironic kidnapper with nonchalant victim,
they go down to the bar together . . .

Monsters of the Deep

We could never understand how it worked:
their relationship was unfathomable.
We told each other Ovidian tales
of blackmail and sinister domination.
Our curiosity was a small boat,
which stopped at a plotted latitude
and dropped anchor, while we projected
ourselves over the side in dry-suits
and bathyspheres, with torches and harpoons,
leaden-footed frogmen of the imagination.

De-militarized Zone

My cigarette glows, and your bones snap
in the dark. Not another torture scene . . .
Like the men in the trenches, I don't smoke,
I don't want to give myself away to the enemy.
—But the tobacco is mixed with saltpetre,
to keep it burning . . . I curse them quietly,
the nervous little cackles of flame in my lap.

It doesn't make sense. You know where I am—
on the chair, carefully holding an ashtray
in my other hand, and listening to you . . .
After our tired argument in your parked car,
we are relaxing from the ordeal of each other;
unwinding, in our different ways.—And you,
you're double-jointed and subject to backache.

I am familiar with your calisthenics,
and the order in which you perform them—
a series of stretches and Yoga positions.
I was told the fluid explodes in the cartilages
and turns to gas. Anyway, it restores you . . .
On good nights, I rub my hands together
and take away the static from your eyes.

Not tonight, of course . . . But even so,
I hear you undressing, in this small room
most of your things land on my feet, and you
get into bed. We weren't talking any more,
but then you ask me to come to bed as well,
and, thinking what a blessing it is to be allowed
to forget our differences like this, I comply.

Body Heat

This evening belongs to a warmer day—
separated clouds, birds, bits of green . . .
We wake late, naked, stuck to each other:
the greenhouse effect of windows and bedclothes.

Fifty years late, you finish *Love on the Dole*.
—Who knows, perhaps it can really be done?
The Boots hair setting-gel no longer works;
your pecker is down. The underdog's leather jacket

is here to stay, the stubborn lower lip
of the disconsolate punk . . . The poor hedgehogs,
they must help each other to pull off the leaves
that covered them while they were hibernating.